A YOUNG READERS TITLE

MY·TEDDY·BEAR

ON VACATION

For a free color catalog describing Gareth Stevens' list of high-quality books, call 1-800-542-2595 (USA) or 1-800-461-9120 (Canada). Gareth Stevens' Fax: (414) 225-0377.

Library of Congress Cataloging-in-Publication Data

My teddy bear on vacation / by Irwin Jorvik, Ltd.; illustrated by
   Anthony Fletcher.
        p.   cm. -- (My teddy bear)
     "First published in Great Britain in 1993 by Kibworth Books,
   Imperial Road, Kibworth Beauchamp"--T.p. verso.
        Summary: Teddy Bear and his toy friends take a train ride to the
   beach and spend the day enjoying the sun, playing in the sand, and
   having a picnic.
     ISBN 0-8368-1539-4 (lib. bdg.)
     [1. Teddy bears--Fiction. 2. Toys--Fiction. 3. Seashore
   --Fiction.] I. Fletcher, Anthony, 1965- ill. II. Irwin Jorvik,
   Ltd. III. Series.
   PZ7.M97859   1996
   [E]--dc20   95-41404

This edition first published in North America in 1996 by
Gareth Stevens Publishing
1555 North RiverCenter Drive, Suite 201
Milwaukee, Wisconsin 53212, USA

First published in Great Britain in 1993 by Kibworth Books, Imperial Road,
Kibworth Beauchamp. Text and compilation © 1993 by Irwin Jorvik Ltd.
Illustrations © 1993 by Anthony Fletcher.

Printed in the United States of America

1 2 3 4 5 6 7 8 9 99 98 97 96

A YOUNG READERS TITLE

MY·TEDDY·BEAR

ON VACATION

Gareth Stevens Publishing
MILWAUKEE

Teddy Bear and all the toys are traveling on a train to the seashore. Wooden Doll is dressed in her summer clothes, and Teddy is wearing a sailor hat. It's a long trip, but there are lots of things to see out the window as the train passes through the countryside.

At last the train arrives at the station. The toys jump down from the car and hurry along the platform. They are in such a rush to get to the seashore that poor Teddy Bear has to carry all the bags. "Wait for me!" he calls.

Toy Soldier and Rag Elephant play in the water. They run across the soft sand and jump in and out of the waves. Wooden Doll and Clown don't like getting wet. Instead, they collect seashells farther up the beach. They place all the shells in a basket.

Rag Rabbit and Rag Doll sit in a large, striped deck chair. They are enjoying the sunshine. It's a little too hot for Teddy, so he sits in the shade under an umbrella.

Here come Wooden Duck and Clown. They want Teddy to play ball with them.

The rock pools are beautiful. The toys can see all sorts of creatures in the water. Toy Soldier notices a crab, and Teddy Bear tries to catch a fish to show to Clown. But the fish hide in the weeds, and they won't be caught.

13

It's time for lunch. Everybody is very hungry. It has been a busy morning. Teddy Bear brought a huge picnic basket full of food. The toys spread a large blanket over the sand. Rag Doll piles lots of sandwiches and cakes on plates. A friendly little dog hopes there will be some left for him.

15

"Let's build a sand castle," says Teddy Bear. "We will build the biggest sand castle on the beach, and you can decorate it with shells," he says to Wooden Doll. Wooden Doll uses the shells that she collected with Clown.

After building the sand castle, Teddy rows a boat on a nearby pond. There's lots of food left over from lunch, and Teddy takes this with him to feed the ducks. He sees many other animals, too, such as butterflies, bright green frogs, and a family of swans.

The toys are hot after digging in the sand. An ice cream treat will cool them off. Clown carries the treats back from the snack stand, but a hungry seagull tries to steal them, and Clown drops them on the beach. They are all covered with sand. Clown will have to go back to the stand to buy some more.

It's time to go home. The toys are exhausted on the short ride back to the railroad station. They have had an exciting day. "I wonder what we will see on the way home," says Teddy Bear to his friends, but nobody replies. They are all fast asleep, dreaming happily about the seashore.

24